Through the Eyes of a Cloud

A Bedtime Story

BY NANCY WILSON WATERS

*Enjoy
& Sweet Dreams
Nancy Waters*

DORRANCE
PUBLISHING CO
EST. 1920
PITTSBURGH, PENNSYLVANIA 15238

Dorrance Publishing Co
585 Alpha Drive
Suite 103
Pittsburgh, PA 15238

Visit our website at *www.dorrancebookstore.com*

ISBN: 978-1-4809-5259-1
eISBN: 978-1-4809-5281-2

Through the Eyes of a Cloud

A Bedtime Story

I dedicate this book to my parents

My Mother, Alice Elizabeth Foss Wilson – her constant caring ways,
fabulous organizational skills, and
vivacious attitude toward life.
From her Red Hat and bridge-playing socials
to the countless hours of her volunteer work.

My Father, Zalph Leon Wilson – a man full of imagination and
the determination and wisdom of five men.
We lost him on the first day of Spring, March 20, 2010, but
he will never be forgotten.

I cannot thank them enough for the
wonderful traits they instilled in me.
I will cherish them for the rest of my life.
July 2015

It was a lovely Spring morning in the wilderness of the great Pacific Northwest.

A beautiful mountain, Mount Hood, stood snow covered and majestic as she looked down over the peaceful little valley of Hood River. The entire sky was blue except for one tiny white puffy cloud. His name was Cloudy.

The forest animals were enjoying their day. Babies were venturing out of their homes and nests, many for the very first time in their lives. Under the watchful eyes of their mothers, a raccoon, some bunnies, twin fawns, robins, and even a family of skunks could be seen in the clearing.

The little white cloud could see all the baby animals scurrying around exploring their new playground. This made Cloudy happy.

A Bald Eagle soared across the deep blue sky and suddenly found himself directly below that little white puffy cloud. The eagle hovered under Cloudy only for a moment, and then quickly sailed away, heading back into the sunshine.

Cloudy wondered why the eagle left so suddenly. He enjoyed being able to gaze at the magnificent bird as the feathers glistened in the sun rays. As the eagle moved across the sky, his wing feathers danced to their own music.

The wildflowers were also waking up from the long winter slumber. It was as if they were stretching their little stem-arms toward the warming sun as it began its climb over the valley.

Small patches of snow now remained where deep drifts once lay across the frozen white fields. Soon those icy patches would melt away to reveal the fertile soil. Then more flowers could grow from their hidden homes to greet the sun.

The sun, too, was happy. It was busy casting warm rays to filter through the tops of the giant evergreen trees. The warmth of the sunbeams eventually reached the forest floor below to be enjoyed by everything the streams of light touched.

Indeed, it was a wonderful Spring day in the Oregon wilderness.

Even the wind appeared as though it had just awakened from its long winter sleep, its strength not yet fully realized. A gentle breeze merely tickled the tops of the gigantic fir trees. The trees looked as if they were giggling as they swayed slightly to the slow movement of the air.

The little cloud saw all of this as he looked down upon the great valley. It delighted Cloudy to watch nature and all of her animals playing and basking in the pleasant sunshine and delicate winds.

Recently the temperatures around the mountain had risen above freezing so that the Spring thaw and runoff could begin.

A nearby brook was making its way down the hill as if it were dawdling, in no hurry at all to get where it was going. Today, all the mountain waterways could enjoy their long peaceful journey to the Columbia River.

Even though it gave Cloudy much pleasure to see and feel the enjoyment among the forest life below, he felt lonely. Everywhere he looked he could see the animals, trees, and flowers enjoying the day. They all had their friends to play with and their families to watch over and protect them.

Cloudy wanted to share in all the joy of the wildlife and surrounding nature. But every time he would move closer to the animals in the valley, he would cast a shadow and they would run away to another sunlit spot.

The sparkling sun was moving toward the western sky, and Cloudy knew that it was coming closer to him. He was thankful to feel the warmth of the yellow beams as they reached out from the brilliant sun.

The puffy cloud thought what a wonderful day it had been in the great valley, even if he wasn't able to play with any of the forest animals. Cloudy knew that, although he was small for a cloud, he was still enormous. He also realized he would probably scare the little creatures if he got too close to them. Cloudy became content to just gaze at the peaceful valley as it came to life beneath him on this beautiful day of Spring.

It had been a busy day for the little cloud. He was able to witness so much beauty, and he sensed the excitement among the forest creatures as they frolicked in the lovely landscape.

Cloudy laughed when he saw the small raccoons chase each other across logs and finally tumble down the hill. He giggled as the bunnies hopped over and around each other and took off running.

As Cloudy watched the twin fawns, he noticed they were very cautious in their new surroundings. They stayed close to their mother while they nibbled on grass and delicate new tree leaves.

The little puffy cloud enjoyed seeing the robins digging through the leaves and grass for worms and bugs to eat. The family of skunks were very busy foraging for a meal under twigs and logs. Cloudy was thankful there was plenty of food for all the creatures in the forest.

As the late afternoon sun continued to warm Cloudy, his little cloud eyes began to close. He remembered the special moments he shared with the wildlife and nature in the beautiful Hood River Valley.

The little white cloud began drifting off to sleep, his head filled with dreams of his wonderful day. For now, he will rest soundly and tomorrow will be another day and a new adventure for Cloudy. Good night, little one . . .

The End